D0295085

Postman Pat
and the Bees

Story by **John Cunliffe**
Pictures by **Joan Hickson**

From the original Television designs by **Ivor Wood**

André Deutsch/Hippo Books

Published in hardback by André Deutsch Limited
105-106 Great Russell Street, London WC1B 3LJ
and in paperback by Hippo Books,
Scholastic Publications Limited
10 Earlham Street, London WC2 9RX

Text copyright © 1989 by John Cunliffe
Illustrations copyright © 1989 by André Deutsch Limited
Scholastic Publications Limited and
Woodland Animations Limited
All rights reserved

ISBN 0 233 98396 1 (hardback)
ISBN 0 590 76185 4 (paperback)

Made and printed in Belgium by Proost

This book is sold subject to the condition that it shall not, by way of trade
or otherwise, be lent, re-sold, hired out, or otherwise circulated without
the publisher's prior consent in any form of binding or cover other than
that in which it is published and without a similar condition including this
condition being imposed on the subsequent purchaser.

"What a lot of bees you have in your garden," said Pat to Mrs. Pottage.

"We just can't get rid of them," said Mrs. Pottage. "There seem to be more than ever, this year."

"You might have a nest," said Pat.

"We might well," said Mrs. Pottage.

A bee came and sat on Pat's nose.
"If you just keep still, it won't hurt
you," said Mrs. Pottage.

But it tickled, and made Pat want to
sneeze. He closed his eyes tightly, and
held his breath, and kept very still.
The bee tickled him with its feet. Then
it flew away.

"It's gone," said Pat.

It buzzed round Jess. He batted at it with his paw.

"Leave it alone, Jess," said Pat, "or you'll get a sting."

"Then we'd have to get the soda," said Mrs. Pottage. "Soda for a bee-sting, vinegar for a wasp."

"I'll remember that," said Pat. "You *have* got a lot of bees in your garden. I'll bet there's a nest in that old tree."

Pat went on his way. The summer was
over. Peter Fogg was getting the last of
the hay in, and the children had all
gone back to school. A bee flew into the
van, and buzzed round Pat's face. He
had to stop to get it out.

"Drat the creature," said Pat. "It
nearly made me go off the road."

Pat could hear the children singing as he went past the school. They sang, "All things bright and beautiful."

"It's a good song," said Pat to Jess. "But I'm not so sure about bees."

Pat had a lot of letters and cards to deliver. There was a flat packet of holiday photographs for the Reverend Timms.

"Aren't these bees a nuisance, Reverend?" said Pat. "I think there's a nest in Mrs. Pottage's garden."

"They're all God's creatures, Pat," said The Reverend. "We'd be badly off without them."

"Well I wish they wouldn't walk on my nose, and buzz about in my van," said Pat.

There was a parcel for Granny Dryden, from her catalogue-place in Manchester.

"Do the bees bother you?" said Pat.

"Not a bit of it," said Granny Dryden.

"Have you ever been stung?" said Pat.

"Lots of times," said Granny Dryden. "It's good for the rheumatics. It doesn't bother me. I can show you one place where I was stung, when I was a girl. It was on the end of . . ."

". . . not on the end of your nose?" said Pat. "I can't see anything."

"No, it was on the end of Blackpool Pier! See, there's the picture over the fireplace."

"Oh, I see," said Pat, laughing.

Pat went on his way. He had six
letters, two magazines, and a post-
card for Miss Hubbard. She had more
bees than anyone. She had thousands!
At the end of her garden were four bee-
hives, and she was busy with them
when Pat arrived. She had a net over
her face, and a thing with smoke
coming out of it.

"Leave the letters by the gate, if you don't want any stings," she called.

"You have to sign for one of them," said Pat. "It's RECORDED DELIVERY."

"Bother," said Miss Hubbard. "Hang on; I'll give them a puff."

She puffed smoke at the bees.

"That'll make them sleepy for a while," she said.

Pat watched from a safe distance.

"That's what Mrs. Pottage needs," said Pat. "I think she has a bees' nest in her old oak tree."

"Has she, now," said Miss Hubbard. "I wonder if that's where some of my bees have gone. I'll ride over and have a look, this afternoon."

Miss Hubbard came to sign for her letter. Quite a lot of bees came with her. "They'll not hurt you," said Miss Hubbard, "if you keep still."

"I wish they'd go somewhere else for a walk," said Pat.

There were six on his hat, three on his neck, two on his nose, and two on his left eyebrow. It wasn't easy for Pat to keep still. He was glad to be on his way.

At Greendale Farm, Miss Hubbard
soon found her swarm of bees, in a
hollow of the tree. Peter Fogg held the
ladder while she climbed up to them.

"Are you sure they won't sting?"
said Peter.

"Just hold that ladder steady, and
you'll be fine," said Miss Hubbard.
"They know me."

She brought them down in an old
shopping-basket, popped them on her
bike, and rode away.

Pat was on his way home when he met Miss Hubbard coming along the road on her bike. She had something in the basket on her handlebars. It was something large and round. Something like a big football.

"Whatever has Miss Hubbard got there," said Pat to Jess. He stopped to see.

"Thanks for telling me," said Miss Hubbard. "I've got them, as you see."

"Got . . . what?" said Pat.

"My bees, of course," said Miss Hubbard.

Pat looked again at her basket. "Bless me!"

He couldn't believe his eyes. What he thought was a big football was really a great ball of bees, humming softly in Miss Hubbard's basket. Pat wound his window up tightly, waved to Miss Hubbard, and drove home.

The next day was cold and rainy, and all the bees stayed in their hives. When Pat called on Miss Hubbard she had two jars of the best honey for him.

"You've earned it," she said.

"Have I?" said Pat. "How?"

"You told me where most of my bees had gone. I had an empty hive ready for them, and I was very pleased to get them back, I can tell you."

"Were they in Mrs. Pottage's tree?" said Pat.

"They were; and they were thinking of staying there," said Miss Hubbard. "All twenty thousand of them."

"And you brought them back on your bike?" said Pat.

"Of course I did," said Miss Hubbard.

"Did you count them?" said Pat.

"No, I just guessed," said Miss Hubbard. "There might have been one or two extra."

"Didn't they sting you?" said Pat.

"Not one of them," said Miss Hubbard.

"Amazing," said Pat.

"Nothing to it," said Miss Hubbard.

"Thanks for the honey," said Pat.

At tea-time, when Pat, and Sara, and Julian had the honey on their toast, what they all said was:

"Delicious!"

It was the best honey they had ever tasted.

"Mmm," said Pat. "It might be worth risking a sting or two to get honey like this."